Also by Jenny Valentine

Iggy and Me

Iggy and Me and the Happy Birthday

Jenny Valentine

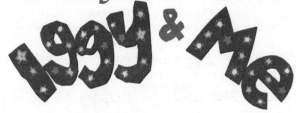
Iggy & Me

ON HOLIDAY

Illustrated by Joe Berger

HarperCollins *Children's Books*

First published in Great Britain by HarperCollins
Children's Books in 2010
HarperCollins *Children's Books* is a division of
HarperCollins *Publishers* Ltd
77-85 Fulham Palace Road, Hammersmith, London W6 8JB

www.harpercollins.co.uk

1

ISBN: 978-0-00-728365-1

Printed and bound in England by
Clays Ltd, St Ives plc

Mixed Sources
Product group from well-managed
forests and other controlled sources
www.fsc.org Cert no. SW-COC-001806
© 1996 Forest Stewardship Council
FSC

FSC is a non-profit international organisation established to promote the
responsible management of the world's forests. Products carrying the FSC
label are independently certified to assure consumers that they come
from forests that are managed to meet the social, economic and
ecological needs of present and future generations.

Find out more about HarperCollins and the environment at
www.harpercollins.co.uk/green

 # Contents

The Last Day of School

It was the end of term for me and my little sister, Iggy.

Iggy didn't want it to be. We were eating our breakfast and she was quite worried.

"Who will look after the hamsters and the guinea pigs?" she said.

"Someone will take the hamsters and the

guinea pigs home," said Mum.

"What will all the teachers do?"

"Someone will take the teachers home too," Dad said. "The teachers will get some peace and quiet."

"What about us?" Iggy said. "What will *we* do?"

"Oh peace and quiet will be off the menu here," Dad said, "that's for sure."

"We'll have fun," I said.

"Flo," Iggy said, like I was being silly. "*School* is fun."

"Holidays are fun too," Mum said. "We'll have a holiday."

"Will we?" said Dad.

"What will we *do* on holiday?" Iggy said,

and she pulled her shoulders up high and her bottom lip down low.

"We'll put you in a dark box and let you out again when school starts," Dad said.

"I don't think so," said Iggy, and she scowled at him.

"We'll get up when we want," I said. "We'll watch telly and wear our pyjamas all day."

"Oh no you won't," said Mum, and Dad said, "Sounds like heaven."

"We'll go out on our bikes," I said, "and have picnics and go to the playground and eat ice cream."

"OK," Iggy said. "That sounds good."

Dad was making coffee and Mum had tea. I ate my toast and Iggy listened to her cereal popping.

"How long is our holiday?" Iggy said.

"Six weeks," Mum said, and Iggy's mouth fell open like a trap door.

"*Six weeks*," she said. "That is *forever*."

"No it's not," Mum said. "It's a month and a half."

"It's forty two days," Dad said, and he looked at us and then at Mum.

"That *is* a long time," Mum said.

"We'll have a nice long holiday," I told Iggy. "You'll see."

On the way to school, Iggy walked extra

fast because she wanted to get there early.

"Hurry up," she said to me and to Mum. "There's only one day left, and it's *now*."

Her extra fast walking made her whole body wiggle and she looked very funny from behind. It made us laugh. But Iggy wasn't laughing. She turned to us and pointed. Iggy only points when she is cross.

"Hurry," she said, pointing, "*Up*."

So we did.

We got to school very early. I took Iggy to her classroom. We were the first people there apart from Rwaida, her teacher. Rwaida was sharpening pencils.

"Did *you* know?" Iggy said, "That this was the last day of school?"

"Yes I did," Rwaida said and she looked happy about it until she saw Iggy's face.

"What will we do for forty-two days and six weeks?" Iggy said.

Rwaida smiled. "We'll think of something," she said, and she dropped the sharpened pencils into a cup with a clatter.

"I hope so," Iggy said. "I hope we do."

It was a good last day of school. We had lessons in the morning like normal. At lunchtime we had foods of the world. We ate things from India and Morocco and France and Somalia and Poland and Bosnia. Most of them were very tasty.

Then we had Golden Time, which is the same as extra play but with a special name.

We could choose football, or aerobics, or making things. I chose making things and so did Iggy. There were jigsaw puzzles and arts and crafts and decorating biscuits. Iggy decorated biscuits. I made a picture for Mum and Dad. I made a beach with blue sea and blue sky, and real sand poured onto glue, and the four of us cut out and stuck there, on holiday.

While I was drawing and cutting and sticking, Iggy came to see what I had made. She had biscuit dust all round her mouth and icing on the ends of her fingers.

"What are you doing?" she said, spraying biscuit dust around.

"I'm making a holiday picture."

"Who's that?" she said, and she wiped her mouth on her sleeve.

"That's you and me and Mum and Dad," I said. "Being on holiday at the seaside."

"What, swimming in the sea and getting shells and making sandcastles?" she said.

"Yep."

"Ooh, I think I like doing that," Iggy said.

"Me too," I said, and we looked at the picture together for a bit longer.

I said, "I'll draw some shells and sandcastles in a minute."

"And starfish," Iggy said. "Draw some starfish and a mermaid."

Mermaids are Iggy's favourite thing to draw and make up stories about. Sometimes Iggy wishes very hard that she was a mermaid. Sometimes she is quite disappointed to have legs.

"Maybe, this holiday," I said, "we could go to the seaside, you and me and Mum and Dad, just

like in the picture. It's *ages* since we've been
to the sea."

Iggy tightened her mouth and shook her
head. She looked very serious and solemn.

"I'm not really having a holiday," she said
in a whisper, like when she tells a secret.

"Why not?"

"Rwaida says she has an important job for
me to do."

"What sort of job?"

"I told you," she said. "An important one."

"I know, but what kind?"

She shrugged. "Rwaida says it is for the
whole summer."

"Oh."

Iggy was still looking at my picture. She

said, "I think I'm going to be a bit busy for the seaside."

I thought about what Iggy's job could be.

"Is it the Guinea pigs?" I said.

Iggy shook her head. "Josh Green's having those."

"Is it the hamster?"

"Nope," Iggy said. "It's not Gruffles."

"Who else?" I said.

"It's not the fish,' she said, "because they get to stay at school and the cleaning lady feeds them."

"Then what can it be?"

Iggy shrugged again and her eyebrows went as high as they could go.

"I don't know," she said. "But I think it must be *very* important."

At the end of the day I waited for Iggy and Mum in the playground. We had to take all of our work home with us, all our books and pictures in a special folder. I had my folder under my arm. It was quite heavy. When Iggy came out of her classroom she had her folder and a little suitcase. She was having trouble carrying it all so I went to help her. I took Iggy's folder and I put it with mine.

"What's in the suitcase?" I said.

Iggy was bursting to tell me.

"It's my job," she said. "Do you want to see?"

We stopped in the playground and I put the folders down. Iggy put the little suitcase on the floor and she fiddled with the clips until it popped open.

"There!" she said.

Inside the suitcase was a bear. Iggy lifted him out. He was brown with a white patch on his eye and a shiny black nose.

"This," Iggy said while the other kids and their mums and dads hurried and chattered around us, "is Barnaby."

"Hello Barnaby," I said, and I pretended to shake his hand. "How do you do?"

Iggy was very pleased with me. She hid behind him and she said, "I'm fine thank you," in a gruff little bear's voice.

Barnaby was wearing trousers and a tiny school jumper, just like the ones we were wearing. There were other clothes in the suitcase too, all folded neatly, and a real camera, the kind you have to throw away when you are finished with it.

"Look at his holiday clothes," Iggy said, and she fished out a little flowery shirt to

 show me, and a baseball cap, and she giggled.

I picked up the camera.

"Don't drop it," Iggy said. "Be careful."

"What's it for?" I said.

"It's Barnaby's camera," Iggy said. "I mustn't lose it."

Just then, Mum came to find us in the playground. She carried our folders and I carried the little suitcase and Iggy carried Barnaby. She put him on her shoulders like Dad carries us sometimes. She held onto his hands just like Dad does.

"Can he see?" she said.

"Yes," I said, and Mum said, "Who is that?"

"It's Barnaby," Iggy said.

"Who's Barnaby?" Mum said.

"He is Iggy's very important summer job," I told her.

"I have to look after him," Iggy said.

"You'll be good at that," said Mum.

"I know. I've got to take him everywhere, and take his picture. And I've got to show all the pictures to the whole class when I get back to school."

Mum laughed. "How lovely," she said.

Iggy said, "So every day he has to do something new and exciting for me to take a picture of."

"OK," said Mum.

"So it's good news," Iggy said.

"What is?" I said.

"About the seaside," Iggy said.

"What seaside?" asked Mum.

Iggy said, "Flo said we could all go to the seaside and I was worried I wouldn't be able to come. I was worried that my job would be too busy."

"I see," said Mum.

"Show Mum your picture, Flo," Iggy said.

I took my folder from Mum and pulled out the picture of us at the seaside.

"There we are," Iggy said. "And now Barnaby can come too."

"I'll draw a Barnaby and stick him on when I get home," I said.

Iggy and Mum smiled at me at exactly the same time.

"Good idea," they both said.

"So you don't mind about the last day of school anymore?" I said to Iggy.

"No," she said. "Not now I've got a job. Not now I've got Barnaby."

"And you don't mind about the long holiday?" I said to Mum.

"No," Mum said and she winked at me. "Not now we're going to the seaside."

Packing

The whole house was turned upside down because we were packing for our holiday at the seaside. All of our rooms were a bit of a mess. Mum was making sandwiches for the journey. Dad couldn't find anything.

"Where are my trunks?" he said.

Iggy giggled. "*Trunks*," she said. "They belong to elephants."

"Well," Dad said. "The particular elephant they belong to is *me*," and he swung his arm in front of his face like a real trunk and chased Iggy across the landing. Iggy squealed and snorted and jumped.

Mum shouted from downstairs, "What's that stomping noise?"

"*Elephants!*" said Dad and Iggy, together.

"Elephants?" Mum said. "Are they coming on holiday with us?"

I said, "Only if they can find their swimming trunks."

"Oh," said Mum, "I see," and she winked at me from the bottom of the stairs.

"Left hand drawer," she called to Dad. "I thought elephants never forget."

"Oh," said Dad. "Thanks. This elephant did."

We had a rucksack each to put our things in. Iggy's was red with white squiggles on it, and mine was blue. Barnaby the bear had his own little brown suitcase with his clothes and his camera in. Iggy had to look after him for the whole summer and take his picture wherever we were. It was the very important holiday job her teacher Rwaida had given her.

I learned all about packing at school. We had a picture of an empty suitcase and we had to draw what we would pack if we had to leave home one day in a hurry. Our teacher said we had to think really hard about what we didn't want to leave behind. She said games and toys and colouring pens were not as important as passports and underwear and important family treasures.

I put all my things on my bed in little piles, like Mum does. We were going to the seaside for six days. I thought very hard about it. I had six pants, six pairs of socks, six T-shirts, two pairs of shorts, one dress, one

pair of jeans and two jumpers. I had my swimsuit and my goggles and my dress that's really a towel. I had my book and my pencil case and my toothbrush and a pack of cards and some yellow sunglasses and a hat with spots on. I did have colouring pens because you never know when you might need to draw a picture. I didn't have my passport because Dad keeps it safe and I didn't have any important family treasures either, but I was all ready to pack.

Iggy came into my room.

"What are you doing?" she said.

She was twiddling her hair. Twiddling hair is Iggy language for

I'm-stuck-and-I-need-help. Iggy has lots of ways of telling you what she is thinking.

She rubs her eyes with her fists when she is tired. Her eyebrows turn bright pink when she is going to cry.

She points when she is cross.

Her mouth goes thin and white when she is angry.

She stretches her arms and points her toes when she is starting to get bored.

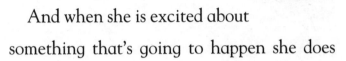

And when she is excited about something that's going to happen she does a little dance with just her hands.

"What are you doing?" she said again, hair-twiddling.

"I'm packing my bag," I said.

"What are you putting in your packing?" she said.

I showed her all the piles of things on my bed.

"That's a lot of stuff," she said, and she stretched her arms over her head and pointed her toes.

"Do you want help with yours?" I said.

Iggy shook her head. "I've done my packing," she said. "And Barnaby's done his."

"What did you pack?" I said.

Iggy counted on her fingers. "Gloria and Mumble and Polly and Ranger," she said.

Gloria and Mumble and Polly and Ranger 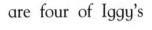 are four of Iggy's best and biggest teddies. They would fill her whole rucksack in a flash.

"What else?" I said.

Iggy shrugged. "Nothing," she said. "No room."

I said, "What about pants and socks and T-shirts and shorts and your swimsuit?"

"I'm wearing them," Iggy said.

I looked at Iggy more carefully. She was looking a bit lumpy.

"All of them?" I said.

"Don't be silly," Iggy said. "I can't wear all of them."

"OK."

"I can only fit four," Iggy said.

She was wearing four pants and two pairs of shorts. She was wearing four T-shirts and a vest and two pairs of socks. She had her swimsuit on all the way underneath.

"What happens if you need a wee?" I said.

"Why?"

"You'll have to take all of it off."

"Why?"

"Because your swimsuit is in the way."

Iggy thought for a minute. "I don't need a wee," she said.

"You will," I said.

"Ssssh," Iggy said. "I don't need one."

"Have you got your toothbrush?" I said.

Iggy nodded. "In my pocket."

"Have you got your sunhat?"

She smiled and showed me. "Other pocket."

Iggy had nearly thought of everything.

"Have you got a book and some pens and a game and a pair of sunglasses?"

"No," Iggy said. "I can't fit them anywhere.

Can I share yours?"

Just then, Mum came into the room.

"Are you all packed?" she said, and I said, "Nearly," and Iggy said, "Yes."

Mum looked at Iggy. She looked at her once and then she looked again.

"Why do you look lumpy?" Mum said.

Iggy smiled like she had a secret she was very proud of.

"What have you got on?" Mum said.

"She's wearing her packing," I told her.

"What does that mean?" Dad said, coming into the room behind Mum.

Iggy twiddled her hair again. She took her sunhat out of her pocket and put it on.

Dad looked at Iggy and frowned.

"What are you hiding about your person?"

"Nothing," Iggy said. "I haven't got a person. I've got Barnaby and he's got his own suitcase and his clothes are too small for me anyway."

Mum lifted up Iggy's T-shirt and found another T-shirt, and then another one, and then another one, and then her swimsuit.

Mum pulled at Iggy's shorts and found another pair, and four pairs of pants, and even more swimsuit.

"Well I never," said Dad.

"What happens if you need a wee?" Mum said.

Iggy crossed her legs. "Don't talk about it," she said.

"You're a human suitcase," Dad said, and Iggy pointed at him.

"No I'm not," she said.

"At least if you fall over on holiday, you won't hurt yourself," he said. "You're all nice and padded."

Mum said, "Why aren't you using your rucksack?"

"It's full," Iggy said. "It's all full up."

"With what?" Mum said.

"Gloria and Mumble and Polly and Ranger," Iggy told her.

GLORIA MUMBLE POLLY RANGER

"The four horsemen of the apocalypse," Dad said.

"No, silly," Iggy said. "They're not horses. They are two penguins and a polar bear and a dog."

"You're right," Dad said. "Yes they are. And they're not coming on holiday with us."

"Why not?" Iggy said.

"Because they are two penguins and a polar bear and a dog."

"Penguins and polar bears like the sea," I said.

"And dogs like the beach," Iggy added.

"They won't like this beach," Dad said, "because they're not coming."

Iggy's eyebrows went pink. "We can't leave them at home," she said. "Barnaby won't have any friends on holiday if we do that."

"Yes we can," said Dad, and Iggy's eyebrows got pinker and pinker.

"I see," Mum said.

"See what?" Dad said.

"The problem," Mum said.

"They want to come too," Iggy said.

"They really want to."

"Oh dear," said Mum.

"Barnaby gets to come," Iggy said, "and it's not fair on the others. And he'll be lonely."

"Never mind," said Dad.

"Can't they fit?" I asked them. "Can't Gloria and Mumble and Polly and Ranger and Barnaby all squeeze in the car with us?"

"No," Dad said. "They're not invited."

"I invited them," Iggy said. "Please can they come?"

"Not really," said Mum.

"Why not?" Iggy said.

"They take up too much room," Dad said.

"We can move up," I told him.

Iggy grinned and nodded and did a little dance with just her hands. "And they can make themselves *really* small," she said. "They squashed right up to fit in my rucksack. They didn't complain."

"Here we go," said Dad.

"Can they?" Iggy said, and I said, "Go on, let them."

I know how much Iggy loves her teddies.

Dad and Mum looked at each other. Mum smiled and Dad blew the air out of his cheeks like a big balloon.

"Just them," Mum said.

"No-one else," Dad said.

"Apart from us," I said.

"Good point," said Dad, and Mum said to Iggy, "Go and take off all that packing and put it in your bag."

"OK," Iggy said, and she ran down the corridor to her room.

"Why the big hurry?" Mum said.

"Can't stop," Iggy shouted back. "Need a wee."

The longest
journey ever

On the day we were leaving for our holiday
at the seaside, we put all our suitcases by the
front door. Our hallway was piled up with
sleeping bags and pillows and teddies and
boxes of food. It looked like we were going
away for ages.

Dad said we should wait while he went

to get the car.

"The car's outside," I said.

"Not that car," he said, and he winked at me. "Our holiday car."

"What's one of those?" Iggy said. "What's a holiday car?"

I didn't know. I didn't even know there was such a thing as a holiday car. I asked Mum.

She said, "Wait and see."

So we did.

Iggy waited by playing with her teddies and asking Mum a hundred times how long Dad would be.

I read a chapter of my book, I watched a cartoon on TV and then I watered all the plants so they didn't get thirsty while we were away.

And after that, we heard a beeping noise outside. It went "Bibbetybibbetybip."

"Is that it?" Iggy said.

"Yes," Mum said. "Come and see."

We went outside and there was Dad, just parking outside, in our holiday car.

It was a yellow van with a white roof. It had windows all around and there were curtains in the windows. They were yellow and white checks.

Iggy did a little dance with just her hands.

"Wow," she said. Yellow is her favourite colour.

Dad's face was in the first window and

was grinning at us. The van made a growling, grumbling, spluttering sort of noise and then it stopped.

"Wow again," I said, and Iggy looked at me and we giggled.

Dad got out and he had to jump down because the van was so high up and then he opened the big door in the side. It slid open with a rolling noise.

"Wow," Mum said.

We couldn't believe our eyes.

Inside, where there are normally just seats, there was a proper room.

From just where we were standing I could see a table and a sofa and some cupboards and a *sink*.

I said to Iggy, "Can you see what I see?" and Iggy said, "Do cars have sinks?" and we laughed again.

We rushed down the path and through the gate for a proper look. A proper look is when you get to touch stuff as well as see it.

"Look at that," Mum said. "It's as neat as a pin."

Iggy snorted. She said, "It's a *lot* bigger than one of those."

"Good," said Mum, "I'm glad, because it's where we're going to be living for the next six nights."

Dad helped us up into the van. He held my hand while I took a really big step and he lifted Iggy right in so she didn't have to climb. Mum and Dad stayed outside and looked in through the open door at us touching everything.

The sofa was soft and foamy and the table was hard and shiny and the cupboards were dark and roomy and the sink was a real life sink. You made the tap work by pressing a thing on the floor with your foot and when you did it right, real water came out. It wasn't easy.

Iggy and I held hands and leaped around with delight. The van rocked like it was a boat on the water.

"Oooh," Iggy said, and she stopped moving. "That feels funny."

Suddenly we saw Dad's legs, and then his feet, and then Mum's face through the back window.

"Come and see," Dad called from somewhere high. "We're up here."

I got down from the van and I helped Iggy down too. We both made an "oof" sort of noise when I caught her.

At the back of the van was a ladder. Mum and Dad had climbed to the top of it and they were looking down at us from the roof.

"What are you doing?" Iggy said.

"Enjoying the view," Mum said.

"What can you see?"

Dad said, "Number fifty-two's grass needs cutting."

Mum said, "Somebody in the next street is having a barbecue."

"Ooh," said Iggy. "I *love* bunbecues. Can we have one?"

"We can," Dad said, "when we get there. We can have one on the beach. Let's go."

Iggy ran to get Barnaby and I went with Mum to get my suitcase. Iggy ran back to the van.

"Come on, Iggy," Mum said, "Come and get your bag," and I said, "It's time to go on holiday!"

"Just a minute," Iggy called. She was taking a picture of Barnaby. He was sitting on the table with his suitcase.

We packed all of our things into the yellow holiday van. It had special compartments for hiding things away so there was room for everything, even the sleeping bags and pillows and boxes of food and Iggy's teddies and Mum's big suitcase.

"What," said Dad, dragging it down the path, "have you got in here?"

"The kitchen sink," Mum said.

"Why do we need another sink?" Iggy said. "We've got one in here."

Mum and Dad sat in the front and we sat behind them in special seats. Iggy's teddies sat with Barnaby around the table like they were having a tea party or waiting for their supper.

"How long till we get there?" Iggy said.

Dad turned and looked at her over the top
of his glasses.

"We haven't even left yet."

"But how long?"

"Three and a half hours," Mum said.
"Maybe four."

"Is that really long?" Iggy said.

Mum said, "It's quite long," and Dad said, "If you're asking already then it's going to be the longest journey ever."

It was funny driving through the streets near our house in a different car. It was like being in disguise. If we had seen someone we knew, they would never have recognised us. Iggy and me wanted to beep and shout and honk and wave because we were so proud to be going on holiday in a yellow van.

Iggy wanted to play her special made-up game that says what animals all the cars are. According to Iggy, some cars look like hippos and some look like panda bears and some look like crocodiles and some look like lizards. Our every day car is a cat because it is black and it purrs and it goes quite fast. The van was louder and clunkier and slower than our car.

I said to Iggy, "If our car is a cat, then what's this van?"

"A tortoise," Dad said, "carrying a bag of spoons."

"A kangaroo,"
said Mum,
"with us in
its pouch."

"No, a secret castle," Iggy said, "on the
back of a rabbit."

Soon we were on the fast roads and all the cars went shooting past us like arrows. I didn't mind how slow or noisy or clunky the van was. It was like driving with our own house, and we'd never done that before.

"We're like a snail," I said, and Iggy agreed.

Dad did something to the van that made it grunt and shudder and he said, "Yes Flo, that's about right."

In our high up holiday van we could see right into other people's cars from above. We saw people eating sandwiches and people reading books and people watching TV and people talking into phones and people picking their noses and people just driving.

To get to where we were going we had to stay on the fast road for a long time. We went right out of the city until everything was just fields. We went over a huge white bridge that looked like a beautiful big ship. Under the bridge we saw where the river turns into the sea. We saw sheep and cows and horses and mountains.

After a while, Iggy started fidgeting.

Her legs twitched, her arms jiggled, her tummy squirmed, her bottom shifted. Even her face didn't want to stay still.

"Ohhhhh," Iggy said.

"What's the matter?" asked Mum.

"I'm all wriggly," Iggy said.

"Do you need the loo?" Mum said.

"I don't know," Iggy said. "Maybe."

"Are you hungry?" Mum said.

"Not sure," Iggy said. "Could be."

"Do you want to stop and stretch your legs?" Mum said.

"Yes," Iggy said, looking down at her knees. "That's what I want to do."

So we stopped in a place for stopping. Dad opened the big sliding door and Iggy jumped out to stretch her legs. She took her teddies with her just in case they wanted to stretch theirs too. We all did a bit of stretching. Then we sat around the table to eat our sandwiches, except for Iggy, who ate hers on the grass with all her toys.

"Isn't this fun," Mum said, and Iggy shouted, "Yes it is!" from where she was sitting.

After we had eaten and stretched and

been to the loo, we all got back in the yellow holiday van. Iggy made her teddies lie down on the sofa for a rest.

"Sleep now, Gloria," she said. "Stop moving about, Mumble. Night, night, Polly. Sweet dreams, Ranger. Stop talking please, Barnaby."

"Hurry up, Iggy," said Dad.

I did up my seat belt and Mum did up Iggy's. The van growled and clunked and grumbled into life. We looked out of the windows at all the new things we could see. The roads were getting smaller and bendier and the hedges were getting higher and higher.

"Won't be long now girls," Dad said.

Mum said, "We're nearly there."

I said, "Let's see who's the first to see the sea," and Iggy giggled because it sounded like a tongue twister. Iggy loves tongue twisters.

We came over the top of a hill, and I was the first to see the sea, all blue and stretching away forever.

"Look, Iggy!" I said. "There it is!"

"Where?" she said, sitting up as high as she could. "Oooh! *There*."

"THE SEA!! THE SEA!!" we shouted together.

When we arrived at the camp site it was almost bedtime. Dad parked in our special spot where we would be staying. We had a good look around, and then Iggy and I put on our pyjamas and went to clean our teeth (outside, in the fresh air, with cups).

When we got back to the van, Iggy stopped suddenly. Her mouth was open in an "Oh!" and her eyes were wide and astonished.

While we had been gone, the van had turned into a bedroom. One big bed had appeared where the sofa and table used to be, and another big bed had appeared in the *ceiling*. The roof had popped up like a jack-in-the-box, all stripy and crumpled. It was amazing. Mum and Dad were sitting on the bottom bed and they were smiling.

"What happened?" said Iggy, and her voice was small with wonder.

"It's bedtime," Mum said.

"How did it know?" Iggy asked.

"How did what know?" said Dad.

"How did the van know it was bedtime?" Iggy said. "How did it *change?*"

Mum blew the hair out of her eyes and laughed, and Dad winked at me. He made his voice small with wonder too.

"We don't know," he said. "It just happened. It's a miracle."

"A *miracle*," Iggy agreed.

"Flo," she said, and she put her hand in mine. "I think our yellow holiday van might be magic."

Mum and Dad slept upstairs, in the ceiling, and we slept underneath.

"We're sleeping in a magic van," Iggy kept saying, and her legs wriggled and her hands danced with excitement.

"No, we're not," said Dad. "We're not sleeping at all."

"Dad," Iggy said, and Dad said, "Yes?"

"You were right," she said. "That was the longest journey ever."

"I agree," said Dad.

"But it was worth it," Iggy said, and Dad turned over in his ceiling bed and said, "Good."

"Magic," Iggy whispered, and then we didn't hear another peep until the morning.

At the Seaside

In the morning, Dad woke us up very early.

I was extremely surprised.

Dad usually likes to stay in bed as long as possible when he is not getting up early for work.

I said, "Why are you up?"

Iggy rubbed her eyes with her fists and said, "I'm still sleeping. I'm not finished."

But when she remembered where we were, she was suddenly wide-awake.

It was warm and cosy inside the van. The sun was shining through the curtains, making everything look yellow, even our faces and hands.

"Oooh," said Iggy, blinking and looking around, "I forgot. We're *here*."

"Exactly," said Dad. "Come and see."

He opened the big sliding door and the air rushed in.

"Brrrrr," Iggy said, "that's *cold*."

"Put a jumper on," Dad said. "Come and get your feet wet in the grass."

The sky was blue and the wet grass was cold and tickly. We could hear the sea shushing and cows mooing and seagulls squawking. We could hear other families waking up at the camp site.

Mum was up already too. She was outside in her nightie and her wellies. She was putting a tiny kettle onto a tiny cooker.

Iggy looked at her and then at me.

"Mum looks funny," she whispered. She put her hand over her mouth and had a secret giggle.

"Good morning," Mum said. "Did you sleep well?"

Iggy kept her hand over her giggle and nodded. I nodded too.

"Yes we did," I said. "Like logs."

"Like dead logs," Iggy said.

We were standing on wet grass in our bare feet and Dad was up early, and Mum was making breakfast in her nightie.

"Aren't holidays fun?" I said to Iggy, "Isn't camping strange?" and she grinned at me and said, "Yes."

We ate cereal and bananas for breakfast and we ate it on a rug, like a picnic. When we climbed back into the van to get dressed, the downstairs bedroom had been put away again. The sofa and the table were back.

"There it goes again," Iggy said. "The magic van. It knew we were up."

"How does it do that?" said Dad, and he winked at me again.

"I've no idea," Iggy said, and her voice was high with surprise. "I haven't got a clue."

We put our swimsuits on and Mum sprayed us with sun cream. It was cold where she sprayed it on and it made us gasp and squirm. It smelled like sweets. Then we got dressed and found our towels and our sun hats. And then we waited for Mum and Dad to be ready. They took ages.

Mum made sandwiches. I helped her wrap them up and put them in a box. Iggy helped too. She counted out four apples, four packets of crisps and five chocolate biscuits.

"Why five?" Mum said.

"Because somebody might want extra," Iggy said.

"Put it back, *somebody*," said Mum.

Dad couldn't find his trunks again.

"I don't want to swim in my knickers," he said, and we screamed with laughter because dads don't have knickers and even if they did they are certainly not allowed to swim in them.

Iggy laughed so much her tummy hurt. And when she stopped laughing she said "knickers" and laughed all over again. She lay back on the grass outside the van and she kicked her legs and rolled over onto her tummy.

"Got them," Dad said, and he held up his swimming trunks.

"What a relief," said Mum.

"Phew," I said.

"*Knickers*," said Iggy, like it was the funniest word ever invented.

We had to walk down a very big hill to the beach. From up at the top we could see the waves coming in and going out. The sand was pale yellow and brown and the sea was blue and grey and white. There were big cliffs all around, and clumps of rocks, and piles of sand as big as hills.

"Dunes," Mum said.

"Like in the desert," I said.

"Exactly," said Mum.

We were carrying our towels and our books and our buckets and spades and Iggy was carrying Barnaby and his camera. It took us a long time to make it to the bottom. Iggy's legs went a bit weak and feeble.

"Are you pooped?" said Dad, and Iggy's legs went even weaker and feebler with laughter.

"Wait till we have to go back up," said Dad, pointing to the top.

"Then I'll be super pooped," Iggy said, and she laughed like crazy at her own rhyme.

The sea was still a long way away. Mum

said the tide was out.

"Where's it gone?" Iggy said.

"I don't know," I said. "Just out."

"So there's more beach for us to be on," said Dad, and he took his shoes off and squidged his toes into the sand.

"Come on," he said, "you do it too."

So we did. We took our shoes off and we squidged. The sand was warm on the top and cold underneath. It was fine and scratchy between our toes. The nearer we got to the water, the wetter the sand felt under our feet.

Mum found a spot for us to put our things. We took off everything apart from our swimsuits and then we raced all the way to the beginning of the sea. The water was cold and swirling and frothy. It was never still.

"Jump!" Dad said when a wave came in and nipped at our ankles. So we jumped.

"Run!" Dad said when a bigger wave

suddenly appeared out of nowhere and tried to get at our knees. So we ran.

We waded out until the water was all the way up to our tummies. The coldness of it made us hold our breaths.

"Swim!" said Dad when the biggest wave of all came rolling towards us, and he dived straight in like a dolphin.

So we swam.

The water was salty and it rushed past my ears and up my nose and when I opened my eyes under there it was all cloudy and green and full of things. Not like a swimming pool at all.

"Ewwww!" shouted Iggy, standing up and spluttering. "There's *stuff* in there!"

"What stuff?" said Mum.

"Plants and stuff."

"Seaweed," I said.

"Ewwww!" shouted Iggy again, and she pulled a face and jumped up and down. "I don't like it!"

"Why not?" said Dad.

"*Slimy*," said Iggy.

"It's just seaweed," Mum said.

"It's all around my legs," Iggy said. She turned and started to wade back towards the sand.

"It's just seaweed and seashells," Mum called after her.

"And fish," Dad said. "And crabs."

"You're not helping," Mum said.

Iggy was still walking.

"And starfish," I told her. "And dolphins," I said.

Iggy slowed down a bit.

"And whales."

I thought hard. "And sunken treasure,"

I said. "And Mermaids."

Iggy stopped. She turned around. "Mermaids?" she said.

I nodded. "Yep. They're in here somewhere."

Mum nodded too, and Dad said, "Definitely."

"Really?" Iggy said. "In here?"

"Yes," I said. "They love seaweed. They eat seaweed like sweets."

"Yuk," said Iggy.

"They like it," I said. "If you were a mermaid you'd think seaweed was delicious."

Iggy has always wanted to be a mermaid. At home she plays mermaids in the bath and at the swimming pool and sometimes even on dry land. She pretends to be a girl with legs who turns into a mermaid whenever she chooses. It is one of Iggy's favourite games.

"We could play mermaids," I said.

"Could we?" Iggy said. She started to hop back towards us.

"We could play it in the sea, where the real mermaids are," I said.

"And treasure?" Iggy said. "Did you say treasure?"

"Yep. Tons of treasure."

"Could we be mermaids finding treasure?" Iggy suggested.

"That's a good idea," I said. "Let's play

mermaids looking for treasure."

"Do you think we'll find some?" she asked.

"We might," I said. "If we keep looking."

"Ok," said Iggy, taking a deep breath before she plunged underwater again. "Let's go."

"Be careful," said Mum.

"And watch out for the *whales*," Dad said, swimming with us, spouting water from between his teeth and splashing his feet like big fins.

We played in the water until we couldn't feel our fingers or toes anymore. Iggy said we must be turning into mermaids for real. Then we got out and lay in the sun.

We made Iggy a mermaid's tail out of sand, right where she was lying.

Iggy took a picture of Barnaby with my
sunglasses on.

We ate our lunch and lazed around and

went for a little explore in the rock pools and sand dunes.

It was a very busy day.

By the time we had walked to the very top of the big hill, everybody's legs were weak and feeble. We had fish and chips in a café and then we went back to the van.

Iggy said, "That was the best day of our holiday so far."

"That was the first and only day of our holiday so far," Dad said.

"True," she said. "But it was still the best. I love the seaside."

"Me too," I said. "I love it as well."

Iggy makes a Friend

Every day at the beach we played mermaids in the sea for so long our fingers and toes went all tingly and blue. Dad was a killer whale and Iggy was the mermaid princess and I was her servant and Mum read the paper.

One day, Iggy wanted to build something

in the sand instead. She wanted to use our buckets and spades and make something amazing, but she didn't know what.

"Let's make a castle for Barnaby to live in," I said.

"King Barnaby," Iggy said. "That's a good idea."

So we got our spades and I drew a big circle around us in the sand and we started to dig a moat. The sun was warm and the sea was shushing and the seagulls were soaring above us in the sky. Our spades made a slicing, sucking sound in the damp sand.

"What's a moat?" said Iggy, digging.

"It's a ditch filled with water around a castle," I told her.

"What for?" she said.

"It keeps the enemy out."

We dug a little bit more.

"What enemy?" Iggy said.

"The invading enemy," I told her. "In the olden days."

"Why does a ditch filled with water keep them out?" she said.

"It's got crocodiles in it," a voice said. It wasn't my voice. It wasn't Iggy's. It wasn't Mum's or Dad's either. They were both lying down with their eyes and their mouths closed.

"Who said that?" Iggy gasped and her whole body went completely still apart from her eyes, which darted about.

"I don't know," I said.

"It was me," the voice said.

It was a little boy's voice. He was behind us. He was peering out over some rocks. He had fiery red hair and hundreds of freckles and a patch of very white sun cream on his nose.

"It's the crocodiles in the moat that get them," he said.

Iggy shuddered. "I hate crocodiles," she said. "They've got too many teeth."

"Hello," I said.

"Hello," said the little boy, and he smiled. He didn't have too many teeth. He had mostly gaps.

"Who are you?" said Iggy.

"I'm Clyde," the little boy said.

"I'm Iggy," Iggy said, and I told him I was Flo.

"What are you doing?" Clyde said.

"Making a castle," I said.

"Making a moat," said Iggy. "But I'm not putting crocodiles in it. Or anything bitey."

"Can I help?" Clyde asked, and he showed us his blue spade and his special silver castle-shaped bucket.

"Yes," said Iggy. "You can *definitely* help. It's for King Barnaby."

"Who's King Barnaby?" Clyde asked, clambering over the rocks towards us.

I pointed to where Barnaby was sitting, on Iggy's towel, in between my mum and dad. Mum was reading and she waved. Dad had the newspaper over his face. I think he was trying to sleep.

Iggy said, "Barnaby is mine. I'm in charge of him. He is my very important job from school."

"Cool," Clyde said, and Iggy grew a little

bit, and she smiled.

Clyde was wearing red shorts and special red beach shoes.

"I like your shoes," Iggy said.

"Thanks," he said. "They're amphibious."

"Cool," Iggy said, and she twirled her hair.

"It means they can live on land and in the water," I whispered.

"I know," Iggy fibbed.

Clyde was good at moat building. He dug and he scooped and he threw the sand into a big pile for making castles with. We had the whole circle done in no time at all.

We stood back to look at our work.

"That was quick," I said.

"Yeah," Clyde said. "We should put crabs in it."

"No," Iggy said. "Please nothing bitey."

"Crabs don't bite," Clyde corrected her. "They pinch, with their pincers."

"Well nothing *pinchy* then," Iggy said.

Clyde frowned. "I put crabs in it before.

It was good."

"When before?" Iggy asked him.

He shrugged. "I've done this loads of times."

"Have you?" Iggy said. "How come?"

"I live here," he said.

Iggy's eyes went as big and round as our moat.

"On the beach?" Iggy said.

"*Near* the beach," Clyde said, scooping some dug-up sand into his big castle-shaped bucket.

"You're lucky," Iggy said. "We just live near traffic lights."

Clyde filled the bucket and then turned it upside down. He tapped the bottom four times with his spade. Then he gently pulled it and underneath was a perfect castle-shaped sandcastle with turrets and windows and archways and a door.

"Wow," Iggy said. "You are *clever*."

She filled our ordinary bucket and she turned it upside down and tapped it, just the way Clyde had. When she gently pulled, underneath was a perfect bucket-shaped sandcastle.

"Not bad," said Clyde. "Not bad at all."

Iggy beamed.

When Mum called us over for more sun cream, Clyde came too.

"Hello," said Mum. "Who's this?"

"It's Clyde," Iggy said. "He's our friend. He's an expert at building castles."

Clyde grew a little bit then too, and he smiled.

"Just look at his bucket," Iggy said.

Clyde held it up for them to see.

"Hello, Clyde," Mum and Dad said.

"Hello."

"He *lives* here," Iggy said. "He lives at the *seaside*."

"That's nice," Mum said.

Dad offered Clyde a chicken sandwich.

"No thanks," said Clyde. "I'm a vegetarian."

"What's one of those?" Iggy said. "Can I be one?"

"It means you don't eat any meat," I told her.

"Ewww, meat, yuk," Iggy said. "I hate that."

This is not strictly true. Iggy likes sausages and roast chicken very much. And she hardly eats any vegetables. She drops them on the floor when Mum's not looking.

She grinned at Clyde and he grinned back.

"How old are you, Clyde?" Mum asked.

"I'm seven," he said, "and a quarter."

"I'm six," Iggy told him, "and a bit."

"Cool," Clyde said.

"Cool," Iggy copied him.

"Cool," Dad said, and winked at me and Mum.

"Who are you here with, Clyde?" Mum asked.

"He's here with me," Iggy said. She was standing very close to him.

"My Mum and Dad are over there," Clyde said, and he pointed.

His mum and dad were quite far away. They were just two little people with a red tent. Clyde waved. They waved back and so did we.

Iggy and Clyde spent the whole afternoon making sandcastles. They didn't stop.

I went swimming really far out with Dad. Mum and I drew an enormous picture of a ship in the sand using sticks. We played noughts and crosses and catch and French cricket. Four times I asked Iggy and Clyde if they wanted to join in, but they didn't. They were much too busy.

When the sun was going down and it was getting colder, they were still hard at work and they hadn't finished.

We packed up our towels and things and we went over for a closer look.

"Time to go, Iggy," called Dad.

"Five more minutes," she said. Clyde

didn't look up from his bucket. His tongue was sticking out and he was frowning with concentration.

Iggy and Clyde hadn't just made a castle for King Barnaby, they had made a whole city.

It was very impressive.

"Brilliant," said Dad.

"It actually is," said Mum.

Clyde's mum and dad had packed up too and they came to see.

"Very good, son," said Clyde's dad. He had fiery red hair and freckles just like Clyde did.

"Very nice dear," said Clyde's mum. She had the same shoes as Clyde, but hers were purple.

"You should take a picture," I said.

Clyde climbed carefully into the middle of the city and placed Barnaby on a castle. Iggy took a picture.

"That's going to be a good one," Clyde said.

I said, "Take one of Barnaby with Clyde."

Clyde stood up dead straight and smiled at the camera.

"Say cheese," Iggy said.

"Cheese."

"Say sausages."

"Sausages."

"Now say Goodnight," Dad said.

"Goodnight," said Clyde.

"I don't want to," Iggy said.

"We've got to go," said Mum.

"But I don't want to," Iggy said.

"Back to the magic van," I said.

Iggy's eyebrows went a bit pink. "I *really* don't want to," she said.

Mum said, "I'm sure Clyde will be back tomorrow, won't you Clyde?"

Clyde looked at his mum and dad. They nodded.

"Yeah," said Clyde.

"So we'll see Clyde tomorrow," Mum said. "OK?"

Iggy looked at Clyde. "Promise?" she said.

"Promise."

"Swear?" Iggy said.

"Swear."

"Can we make castles again?" Iggy said.

"Yeah," said Clyde. "And I'll show you a starfish if you want."

Iggy smiled. She beamed. She puffed up. "I do," she said in squeaky little voice. "I do want."

"See you tomorrow," I said.

"Cool," Clyde said.

"Yeah, cool," said Dad.

All the way up the hill, Iggy talked about Clyde. She talked about him while we ate our supper, and afterwards while we played hopscotch, and when we were cleaning our teeth. She talked about him after Mum and Dad had closed the curtains and kissed us goodnight.

She said, "Clyde is so clever," and "Clyde is quite tall."

She said, "Clyde's teacher is called Mrs Jones."

She said, "Clyde's bucket is the best bucket I've ever seen."

She said, "Clyde is going to show me a *starfish*."

She said, "Clyde is my best friend."

Dad said, "Clyde is asleep and so should you be."

Iggy said, "Night, Mum. Night, Dad. Night, Flo,"

"Night, Iggy," we all said, and we counted to ten in the silence before Iggy spoke again.

"Night, Clyde," Iggy said.

Where Is Iggy?

"Wow," said Iggy. "Today is *busy*."

We were standing at the top of our hill before the long walk down to the beach. We couldn't just see the blue and grey sea and the yellow and brown sand and the black and grey rocks. Today we could see all the colours of the rainbow. We could see umbrellas and tents and towels and rugs and

swimsuits and people and dogs and flags and
kites and beach balls and surfboards. Our
beach was packed.

"It's rush hour," Dad said.

"It's Saturday," said Mum.

"It's *crowded*," said Iggy. "How will we find
Clyde?"

"Don't worry," I told her. "I'll help you."

We went to our usual spot but it was full
of another family. We went to the spot

where Clyde's mum and dad usually sat, but that was full of another family too. In the end, Dad found a nice sheltered patch in a dune. The sand was dry and golden and dusty. When the wind blew, the sand blew too. It stuck to the sun cream on our arms and legs and faces.

"Ooh," said Iggy. "I'm all scratchy."

"Like sandpaper," Dad said.

"Like sand*people* you mean," said Iggy.

It was hot and cosy in the dunes and Mum and Dad lay down with their eyes closed, even though we really hadn't been out of bed for that long.

"Can we go the sea?" I said.

"You can paddle," said Mum. "But don't

swim. Not without us."

"OK," I said.

"Promise?" Mum said.

We promised.

"Can we take Barnaby?" Iggy said. "He hasn't been for a paddle yet."

"I'm not sure he'll like it," Dad said.

"Oh, I think he will," said Iggy.

"Well don't drop him in," Mum said. "I don't think he can swim."

We walked down to the water. Iggy held my hand so she could look for Clyde while she was walking, instead of where she was going. She had

Barnaby tucked safely under her other arm. He was wearing his flowery holiday shirt and a tiny pair of white shorts.

"I can't see Clyde," Iggy said. "He's not here."

"Maybe he's in the water," I told her. "Or maybe he'll be here later."

The water was very crowded too. All along it there were people paddling and splashing and squealing and shouting. I held tight to Iggy's hand and she held tight to Barnaby and we put our feet in. It was cold and frothy again and it was also thick and brown with churned up sand from so many paddlers.

"Oh, look," said Iggy.

A little dog was standing next to Iggy with its feet in the water just like us. It was sniffing at Barnaby's paws.

Iggy loves dogs. She bent down to stroke it
and I bent down to look at its collar.

"Spencer," I read. "His name is Spencer."

"Hello, Spencer," Iggy said, picking up his
paw and shaking it, like it was a real hand,
like they were saying how do you do.

Spencer was brown and white and grey and he was dripping wet and he had sand in the fur all round his mouth.

"Awww," Iggy said. "Is your beard all sandy?"

Spencer had a green ball. He dropped it in the water at Iggy's feet and then he jumped and barked for her to throw it.

"OK," said Iggy, "Fetch!" and she threw the ball into the water. The little dog hopped and bounced over the shallow waves to get it. He brought the ball back to Iggy again. He dropped it and barked.

"Good boy, Spencer," Iggy said. "Fetch it, Spence."

She threw the ball the other way this time,

to trick him. Spencer darted into the water and then spun around and darted out towards where it rolled, green and covered in sand. He picked the ball up with his mouth and all the sand went in his nose and made him sneeze.

"Bless you," Iggy said, tucking Barnaby into her armpit and rubbing Spencer's sandy wet ears and talking into his neck.

Spencer sneezed again twice.

"Bless you, bless you," Iggy said.

Spencer shook the sand and the water off himself. He started at his face and he twisted and wiggled all the way from the tip of his nose to the end of his tail. Last of all he shook his bottom. Specks of sand and drops

of salty water flew off him in all directions.
Iggy thought it was the funniest thing she
had ever seen.

"Do it again, Spence!" she squealed, and
she held Barnaby up to see.

Spencer put the side of his head on the
sand and then his shoulder and then he lay

down and rolled onto his back so we could see his scruffy, tufty fur and the pink skin on his belly. He stuck his legs in the air and he rolled about, like he was having a good back scratch. I could see all of his teeth. He looked like he was laughing.

"What's funny, Spencer?' Iggy said, lying down on her back in the sand next to him. "What's so funny boy, eh?"

Iggy picked up the ball and threw it again, further away from the sea. Spencer scrambled up and chased off after it. I turned to look at the sky and at all the people bobbing up and down in the water and when I turned back, Iggy was gone.

"Iggy?" I said. I looked for her pink and

blue and yellow swimsuit. I looked for her red and white striped hat. I looked for Barnaby's flowery shirt. I looked for Spencer and his green ball. I couldn't see any of them. All I could see was other people. Big people and little people, fat people and thin people, brown people and white people and sore pink people. All I could see was legs and arms and tummies and faces and none of them belonged to my little sister and her teddy bear or a little dog.

"Iggy?" I said again, louder. "Where are you?"

Iggy didn't answer.

I stood completely still for a minute and I watched very carefully to see if she was coming back.

She wasn't.

I was a bit scared.

I wanted to go and get Mum and Dad but I didn't know if I should move.

What if Iggy came back and I had gone? What would happen then?

I was rooted to the spot.

"IGGY!!" I shouted one more time, at the top of my voice.

Still no answer.

Just when I was about to give up hope, I saw Mum and Dad, walking down the sand towards me. I jumped up and down and waved. I ran a bit towards them and then back to the water, just in case.

"Hello," Dad said. "Are you OK?" and Mum said, "Where is Iggy?"

I told them what happened. I said, "I turned away for a second and Iggy and Spencer disappeared."

"Who is Spencer?" asked Dad.

"He's a little dog," I said. "With a green ball. He and Iggy were playing."

Mum and Dad stood by the water and looked just like I did. They shouted for Iggy just like I had. All they could see was people, just like me.

"What are we going to do?" I said.

I was worried about my sister. Iggy wouldn't like being lost.

"Don't worry," said Dad. "Keep looking. We'll find her."

I kept looking but I couldn't see her. I didn't know if we would find her or not.

"Which way did she go?" said Mum.

"She threw the ball that way," I showed her, pointing.

"Right," she said.

Dad said to Mum, "You go that way and I'll check the shoreline."

He said to me, "You stay there, Flo. Don't move a muscle."

I stood with my feet in the water and I

didn't move. I kept my eyes peeled for a little brown and grey and white dog with a green ball and a little girl with blonde hair wearing pink and blue and yellow and red and white. I just couldn't see them.

Wherever Iggy was, I hoped she wasn't as sad and as scared and as worried as me.

"Any luck?" said Dad when he walked back to where I was waiting. "Have you seen anything?"

I shook my head and I felt like crying. But just then, I spotted a flash of grey and brown and white dog, hurtling across the sand.

"That's Spencer!" I said to Dad.

I called him, "Come here, Spencer, come here boy."

The little dog ran towards us. I could see even from a distance that he didn't have a green ball in his mouth anymore. He had Barnaby.

Dad got him by the collar and pulled the bear out of his jaws. Barnaby was a bit soggy and sandy and crumpled, but he was all right.

I hoped Iggy was all right.

I ruffled Spencer's wiry head.

"Where's Iggy, Spencer?" I said. "What have you done with her?"

Spencer barked and jumped and snapped at Barnaby's paws.

"Where is she, boy?" I said. At that moment, I wished dogs could talk more than I'd wished for anything else in my life. I wished Spencer could say, "She's over there behind those rocks and she's been looking for you but she's all right."

But all Spencer did was bark and jump and snap. He got to his feet, and he scratched his tummy with his back leg, and then he ran off.

I watched him go, and through the crowds I caught sight of someone I knew.

"Clyde!" I called and I waved at him with both my arms.

Clyde was wearing blue shorts and a blue cap and he had on his red amphibious shoes.

"Hello," he said to me and Dad. "Iggy's looking for you."

"Where is Iggy?" I said, and Dad said, "Have you seen her?"

Clyde nodded. "She got lost," he said. "She's with my Mum and Dad. They sent me to find you."

"Well, what a relief," said Dad.

Mum came back pretty soon, looking worried, but when she saw Clyde, and the smiles on all our faces, she started smiling too.

Clyde took us to where Iggy was. She was a bit sniffly and she was pleased to see us. She was very pleased to see Barnaby, too. We all had a big hug.

"We were a bit worried," Mum said.

"I followed Spencer," Iggy said. "And then he stole Barnaby. And I got lost. And then I found Clyde."

"That was very lucky," Mum said.

"Yes," I said. "You wanted to find Clyde today, didn't you?"

"And we're glad you did," Dad said, and he said thank you to Clyde's mum and dad as well, for helping.

"Clyde rescued me," Iggy said. She put her head on Clyde's shoulder and she sighed.

"You're a hero, Clyde," Dad said. "You rescued a damsel in distress."

"A what?" said Clyde and Iggy said, "What did you call me?"

"A damsel in distress," said Dad. "A lady in a pickle. A girl who needed help."

"Oh," said Iggy, "OK."

"Oh," said Clyde. "Cool."

A rainy day

One morning when we woke up in the van, it wasn't all warm and cosy and yellow. It was cold and dark and it sounded like someone was dropping wet marbles onto our roof.

It was raining.

"Oh, joy," said Dad.

Mum hoped it was just a shower, but when

we opened the curtains for a look, the sky was very low and angry and grey. There wasn't a glimpse of blue. There wasn't a peep of sunshine. All the tents and cars and vans looked sad and huddled in the wind and the rain. There weren't any people. Everything was dripping.

"What will happen to the beach?" Iggy asked.

"Nothing," said Dad. "It will be empty. It will just get wet."

"It already *is* wet," Iggy said.

"Good point," said Dad.

"What will we *do* all day?" she said, and she stretched her arms and pointed her toes. That's what Iggy does when she is bored, and being bored was what Iggy was worried about.

"Nothing," said Dad. "Not a thing."

Iggy stretched and pointed even harder.

"That's not true," Mum said. "There are lots of things we can do."

"Like what?" Iggy said.

"We can read," Mum said. "And we can draw and listen to music. We can have a walk."

"Out *there?*" Iggy said, and she pointed at the fat lines of rain slithering down the windows.

"Yes, out there," Mum said. "With our

waterproof coats and wellies on."

"We can take more pictures of Barnaby," I said, "in all his holiday outfits. We can take pictures of him making lunch and doing the washing up and reading a book."

"Mmmm," Iggy said, thinking. "We could do that."

"We can do lots of things," Mum said. "You'll see."

We ate our breakfast at the table in the van instead of outside on a rug. There wasn't much room. Everybody was all elbows.

Dad told Iggy to move her teddies before he moved them for her.

He said, "I don't want to sit on two penguins while I'm eating my cornflakes."

Iggy said, "Gloria and Mumble don't want to be sat on by *you*," and she put them on her lap. She couldn't reach her cereal with them in the way. The milk splashed off her spoon and onto her pyjamas.

"Watch it, cheeky," said Dad.

Mum took Gloria and Mumble and Polly and Ranger and Barnaby out of our way and put them on Dad's driver's seat.

"Now they can pretend they are going on an adventure," I said.

"Good idea," said Iggy. "I'm going to do that with them after breakfast."

It was a bit of a squish getting dressed as well. Dad banged his head on the ceiling twice.

"Ooof," he said, and Iggy giggled.

"Ouch!" he said, and she sniggered.

"Not funny," he said, and she rubbed his head better for him and kissed it.

"A bit funny," she said.

Mum and Dad washed up at the sink and Iggy dried and I put things away. We whistled while we worked. Dad whistled and Mum hummed and Iggy tra-la-laad and I tapped my foot.

"Now what?" Mum said.

"I'm going to Butterfly World," said Iggy.

"What?" Dad said, and "How?"

"I'm driving there," Iggy said, getting into Dad's driver's seat and putting on his seat belt, "with my Teddies."

"Oh, yes," Dad said, "Of course."

"What *is* Butterfly World?" asked Mum.

Iggy told her it was a magic place filled with all the trees and plants that butterflies especially love.

Dad said, "In real life it would be a clump of buddleia and a café and a gift shop."

"What's buddleia?" I said.

Mum said, "It's a plant that butterflies especially love."

Iggy said, "We will walk around in there and all the butterflies will come and land on our hands and our heads and our shoulders. They will fly about our faces."

"Sounds good," I said. "Sounds nice and tickly."

"Do you want to come?" asked Iggy. "Hop in."

I climbed into Mum's seat and Iggy said, "Put your seat belt on," just like Mum does, every time we get in the car. Then she pretended to drive with all the teddies on her lap. She made engine noises and she turned the steering wheel about.

"You're a very good driver," I said.

"Thanks."

"How long till we get there?" Dad shouted from the back, and Iggy turned and grinned at him.

"A hundred and forty-two hours," she said.

"Good," Dad said. "I can read my book for a bit then."

Iggy pretended to drive for ages. I breathed on my window and wrote my name and drew some hearts and butterflies and stars.

Suddenly I had an idea.

"I know, Iggy," I said. "Let's make Butterfly World for real."

Iggy didn't take her eyes off the road. She frowned. "How?"

I leaned over and whispered into her ear.

"Oooh," she said, and then she made the sound of screeching brakes.

"Are we there?" Mum said.

"Not yet," Iggy said.

"Not quite," I told them.

"Mum," I said. "We need your help."

"What for?"

"It's a secret," Iggy told her.

"Right," said Dad. "I'll take my book upstairs to bed then."

"Thanks," I said.

"It's my pleasure," he grinned.

Dad climbed up into his bed. He moved

about a bit getting comfy. There wasn't much room between him and the roof.

"Are you all right up there?" Mum said. "Can you see?"

"Never been better," Dad called down. "And I can see perfectly well if I remember to keep my eyes open."

Mum smiled. She whispered to me and to Iggy, "He'll be asleep in a minute."

Mum helped us to get our pens and paper out of our bags in the cupboard. She found some scissors and she even had some glitter and ribbon and stickers and glue that she had brought with her.

"For a rainy day," she said, and Iggy said, "Well, that's lucky."

144

"Do we have any cotton?" I said.

"Cotton?" said Iggy.

"Thread," I said. "For hanging."

Mum said she didn't think so, but that when we were finished we could put our coats and wellies on and go the camp site shop.

"That can be our walk," Iggy said. "To the shop."

"They'll have some thread there," Mum said.

"And ice lollies," Iggy said. "They'll have ice lollies too."

"Will they?" said Mum and Iggy nodded.

"Well then maybe we'll get some," Mum said, and Iggy smiled.

We sat at the table together and we made
butterflies. This is how we did it.

Mum tore the paper into all different sizes.
I folded each piece exactly in half and drew
half a butterfly on one side. Iggy kept the

paper folded and did the cutting. Iggy loves scissors. She cut the half butterflies out very, very carefully and when she unfolded the paper there was a whole butterfly, every time. Then we drew and cut and stuck and glittered them until we had loads and loads of butterflies, all landed on our table.

"Listen," Mum said, when we were busy in the middle of doing it. Iggy stopped cutting and Mum stopped tearing and I stopped colouring.

We listened.

Dad was snoring, ever so gently.

"Like a baby piglet," said Iggy.

We put our waterproof things on as quietly as we could, which was not very.

"Sssh," said Mum, and Iggy said she couldn't. It was impossible.

"Waterproof clothes make too much noise all by themselves," she whispered.

We put our boots on and we climbed out of the front door instead of the side one because it was quieter. Then we trumped and traipsed through the wet puddly grass to the camp site shop. Our boots made a sucking noise and the grass went all flat and squashed where we trod. The rain pitter-pattered on our waterproof clothes and landed all cold on our faces.

The shop was tiny and full of all the things
you might forget to bring on holiday. Like
batteries and teabags and orange juice and

dog food, and thread. Mum bought some and she told us we could have an ice lolly too, if we wanted.

"It's too cold," we said, and Iggy said, "I'd rather have a hot chocolate."

So mum bought some hot chocolate as well, to make on the tiny stove, with the tiny kettle.

We trumped and traipsed back through the rain to the van.

Dad was still snoring.

"He's still fast asleep," Mum said.

"Yep," I said. "And when he wakes up, he will be in Butterfly World."

We gave each butterfly a little piece of

thread and we tied them all around the van, on the door handles and the ceiling and the driving mirror and the steering wheel. On the cupboards and the window catches and the seats and the tap. Iggy tied one to each of Barnaby's ears. She tied one to Gloria and Mumble and Polly and Ranger. We tied them into our hair. We tied them *everywhere*.

Soon the whole van was alive with fluttering, dancing butterflies. Every time we moved, they moved too. If you blew on them or waved at them their little wings shivered and shook.

Mum made hot chocolate for us, and tea for her and Dad. The butterflies trembled in the steam from the tiny kettle.

She climbed up to where Dad was sleeping.

"Wakeywakey," she said. "Rise and shine."

Dad came down with his face all creased and his hair all sticking out and his eyes all puffy. As he moved through the van, the butterflies flipped and dived and

cartwheeled. He looked around and his face
woke up with wonder.

"Am I still dreaming?" he said.

"Nope," said Iggy, and she did a little
dance with just her hands.

"Then where am I?" Dad asked.

"Butterfly World," said Iggy. "We made it
especially for you."

Iggy and Barnaby

On our first day back at school after the holidays, Iggy got up and dressed and ate her breakfast much slower than normal.

When Mum woke her up, Iggy said, "Not finished," and she rolled over for a bit more sleep.

Our school uniform was folded on our beds and our hairbrushes were where we could see them, but Iggy came down to breakfast in her pyjamas with her hair facing in all directions.

"Good afternoon," Mum said. "You look very smart."

Iggy growled.

"Not ready," she said.

"What's the rush?" said Dad, as Iggy put rice puffs into her mouth, one at a time, as slow and as sleepy as a sloth.

Iggy's eyes were hardly even open.

"There isn't one," I told him.

"Are you tired?" Mum said, and Iggy said nothing.

"Are you feeling all right?" Dad said, and Iggy shrugged.

I said, "You normally like to get to school nice and early."

"So early that it's still closed," Dad said. "So early that there's nobody there."

Iggy glared at him over the top of her spoon.

"The teachers are there," she said. "Teachers are allowed to be at school as early as they want."

"Lucky them," Dad said.

Iggy ate one rice puff.

Mum said, "You're not going to be early if you're still in your pyjamas."

Iggy shrugged. "I don't want to be early. I don't want to go."

Mum stopped smiling and Dad stopped stirring his coffee and I stopped buttering my toast.

Iggy had never said she didn't want to go to school before.

It was a first.

"Say that again," Dad said.

"I'm not going," Iggy said, and she put her spoon down and looked at the rice puffs floating in her bowl.

"Well that's a shame," said Mum, getting up from the table and opening the fridge. "I was just about to put your favourite yogurt in your packed lunch."

Iggy looked at the yogurt. She shrugged again. "Not going," she said.

"Why not, Iggy?" I said.

"I don't want to."

I looked at Iggy and Mum looked at Dad and Dad looked at me.

"Oh dear," Mum said.

"I didn't know it was that easy," Dad said.

"What?" Iggy said.

"Not doing things," he said. "I didn't know you could just not want to."

"What do you mean?" I said.

Dad stretched his arms over his head. "I'm not going to work today," he said.

"Why not?" Mum asked him.

Dad shrugged. "I don't want to."

Mum said, "I don't think I'll do any work today either. I don't think I'll do anything at all. I'm not making anyone any supper."

"Why not?" Dad said, and Mum smiled. "I don't want to," she said.

"What about you, Flo?" Dad said. "What are you not going to do today? Are you not going to say the word banana a hundred times? Are you not going to eat only carrots?

Are you not going to hop on one leg and flap your arms instead of walking?"

"No," I said. "I'm not going to do any of those things."

"Why not," said Dad. "Don't you want to?"

Iggy didn't even smile. She twirled her hair and looked glum.

"Did you know," Dad said in a quiet and serious voice like he was telling a secret, "that not going to school is against the law?"

"No," said Iggy.

"Yes it is," said Dad. "And if you don't go, they'll send a policeman round here to arrest your mother."

Iggy looked at Mum and then at me. She

twirled her hair furiously.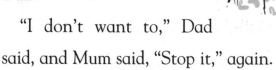

"Stop it," Mum said to
Dad.

"I don't want to," Dad
said, and Mum said, "Stop it," again.

"I don't think that's true," I said. "That's
not true is it Mum?"

"It's not true," Mum said. "So don't worry.
Finish your breakfast."

I put my plate in the sink and Iggy drank
a little sip of her juice and wiped her orange
mouth on her sleeve.

"Come on you," said Mum, holding out
her hand to take Iggy upstairs. "Let's go and
see what we can do."

I brushed my teeth and I put my books and

pens in my bag and I got my packed lunch and my drink. Then I waited by the front door. Mum and Iggy were a long time. After a while, I started looking at where my watch would be if I was wearing one.

"Come on," I said. "Hurry up."

"I think we're ready," Mum said, and she and Iggy came slowly down the stairs.

Iggy looked dressed and brushed and ready but she didn't look happy.

"Got everything, Iggy?" I said.

Iggy shrugged.

"Let's go," I said.

I liked the walk to school because we hadn't done it in ages. All the things I looked at seemed new, even though we had

seen them all before. We walked down our
road and round the corner and up the hill
and over the railway bridge and then we
were nearly there. Lots of other children
were walking to school with their mums and
dads. Everyone looked neat and tidy and

excited for the first day of a new term. Everyone except for Iggy. She scuffed her shoes and dragged her feet and she wouldn't walk faster than a snail, even though we asked her.

"Come on, Iggy," Mum said. "You're going to be late."

"Catch up, Iggy," I said. "You're getting left behind."

Mum said to Iggy, "Your class will be so excited to see what you and Barnaby have been up to all summer," and when she said it, Iggy stopped dead in her tracks.

"What?" said Mum.

"Have you got Barnaby?" I said.

Iggy shook her head.

"Did you leave him at home?" I said.

"You didn't?" Mum said.

Iggy nodded and I said, "She did."

"And all the photos?" Mum asked. "All your lovely pictures?"

Iggy nodded again.

"Oh dear," said Mum, and Iggy's eyes got sadder and her eyebrows got pinker and her chin began to wobble. Iggy's chin wobbles when she's trying really hard not to cry.

Poor Iggy. All holiday she had remembered Barnaby. She had kept him safe in the van and dry at the beach and she had brought Gloria and Mumble and Polly and Ranger along to keep him company. She had shown him the sea, and built him a castle and let him touch an ice cream, and every day she

had taken pictures of him to show her class. She hadn't forgotten him once.

Until today.

I felt very sorry for her.

"What shall we do?" I said. "Can we go back and get him?"

Mum looked at her watch. "I don't think we've got time," she said.

"What if we run?" I said.

"We might make it," Mum said. "If we hurry."

"I'm not going," Iggy said, and her voice was all husky.

"Not going where?" I said. "Not going to get Barnaby or not going to school?"

"Not doing either," Iggy said.

"You have to," Mum said.

Iggy shook her head and planted her feet.

"I'm not going," she said. "I'm staying here."

"Why?" I said. Iggy shrugged.

Mum took a deep breath in.

"Iggy, you can't do that," she said.

Iggy kept her feet planted and she stuck out her chin and closed her eyes. Sometimes when you say something to Iggy that she doesn't want to hear, she closes her eyes and pretends you're not there. Mum doesn't like that.

"Iggy," said Mum. "I'm warning you."

Iggy closed her eyes even harder.

"I'm going to count to five," Mum said.

I hate it when Mum counts to five. I had to think of something, quick.

"I know," I said. "I've got an idea."

Mum stopped counting and Iggy stopped closing her eyes, and they both looked at me.

I said, "If we have Barnaby at home for one more day we can have a special goodbye party for him."

Iggy looked at her feet.

"Good idea," said Mum. "Keep talking."

"Well," I said. "We could make a banner and have a cake and we could say goodbye properly to Barnaby. He's been with us all summer. I know Gloria and Mumble and Polly and Ranger are going to miss him."

Iggy said, "I'm going to miss him too."

Her eyes were sad circles and her mouth was a thin white line.

And then I knew why Iggy didn't want to come to school. And I knew why she had left Barnaby behind, too.

Iggy hadn't forgotten about him, of course she hadn't.

Iggy hadn't forgotten about Barnaby all summer. She just didn't want to give him back.

She didn't want to say goodbye.

"It'll be all right, Iggy." I said. "We can

have a nice party for him. And you'll see him at school."

Iggy's feet came unstuck from the pavement. She sniffed and she smiled a bit and she shuffled slowly towards us.

"Can we have a party?" she said, and Mum gave her a hug and said, "Yes."

We carried on walking behind Iggy to school. Mum took my hand and whispered, "Nice one, Flo."

Mum explained to Rwaida, Iggy's teacher, that Barnaby was not quite ready to leave yet, but that he and his holiday pictures would be there in the morning.

"That's fine," Rwaida said and Iggy smiled with relief. "He's probably just sleeping off his busy summer."

"Yes," Iggy said. "He is."

That afternoon when we got home from school, we made a GOODBYE BARNABY banner. We stuck bits of paper together with sticky tape until they were long enough to fit all the words and we put it on the wall in the kitchen.

Mum found some paper party plates and cups and napkins in the cupboard, left over from Iggy's birthday. We had sandwiches and biscuits and glasses of milk. Iggy made a space for Gloria and Mumble and Polly and Ranger at the table. And she made a special

seat for Barnaby by piling all our cushions onto a chair so he could reach.

When Dad came home from work he said, "Is it somebody's birthday? Have I forgotten somebody's birthday?"

"No," I said, and Iggy told him it was just Barnaby's goodbye day.

"Ah," Dad said, stroking Barnaby's ear and kissing Iggy on the top of the head.

"Goodbye, Barnaby."

"Goodbye, Dad," Iggy said in her gruff little bear's voice. "Goodbye, everyone."

About the author

Jenny Valentine moved house every two years when she was growing up. She worked in a wholefood shop in Primrose Hill for fifteen years where she met many extraordinary people and sold more organic loaves than there are words in her first novel, *Finding Violet Park*, which won the Guardian Children's Fiction Prize. The *Iggy and Me* books are her first titles for younger readers.

About the illustrator

Joe Berger grew up in Bristol, where he did an Art Foundation Course before moving to London in 1991. He works as a freelance illustrator and animator, and also co-writes and illustrates a weekly comic strip in the *Guardian*. His first picture book, *Bridget Fidget*, was nominated for the Booktrust Early Years Award.

More stories about Iggy and me: